What can you do with a shoe?

What can you do with a shoe?

by **Beatrice Schenk de Regniers**

pictures by **Maurice Sendak**

MARGARET K. MCELDERRY BOOKS

MARGARET K. McELDERRY BOOKS

25 YEARS • 1972–1997

An imprint of Simon & Schuster Children's Publishing Division
1230 Avenue of the Americas
New York, New York 10020

Printed in the United States of America
First Edition
10 9 8 7 6 5 4 3 2 1

Library of Congress Catalog Card Number: 96-20871
ISBN 0-689-81231-0
ISBN 0-689-81597-2 (Limited Edition)

This is the first edition of *What can you do with a shoe?* to have full-color illustrations.

for fun

What can you do

What can you do

What can you do

with a shoe?

You can put it on your ear

On your beery-leery ear,

You can put it on your ear, tra-la

Or wear it on your head

Or butter it like bread

Or use apple jam instead, ha ha

Oh, stop all that nonsense!

What do you *really* do with your shoes?

Of course!

What can you do

What can you do

What can you do

with a chair?

You can pretend you are a bear   saying boo   in a zoo

Or a seasick kangaroo   (Now the chair is a canoe)

Or use it for a table
When you're sitting on the floor

Or if you are able
Shove it up against the door

So *nobody* can get in unless you say so.

Or it's an airplane

Or a train

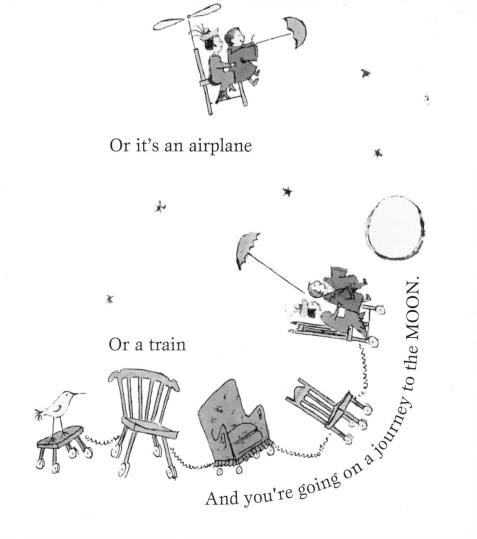

And you're going on a journey to the MOON.

Now Really!

Is that what you're *supposed to do*
    with a chair?

What do *most* people do with chairs?

That's right!

What can you do   What can you do   What can you do   with a hat?

You can fill it up
  with pickles

Or with popcorn

Or with glue.

An octopus could rest in it

A bird could build a nest in it

A turtle be a guest in it. . . .

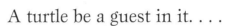

Or would a horse look best in it?

Oh, don't be so silly!
What *do* you do with your hat?

Just what everybody does!

What can you do   What can you do   What can you do   with a cup?

You can gobble it up!

Gobble gobble gobble   gubble gubble gubble

Crunch!

Yummy! What a lunch!

Who ever heard of eating cups for lunch?
     Or even for breakfast?
You know what people do with cups,
     don't you?

Drink milk

Or tea

Or coffee

Or orange juice.

Things like that.

Now that makes *sense!*

What can you do
What can you do
What can you do

with a broom?

You can use it for a hair brush

Or a tooth brush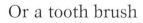

Or a bear brush
(If you've got a bear)

You can use it for a shoe brush

Or a glue brush

Or a chair brush
(I'm sure you've got a chair)

Now a broom would feel real tickly
to a prickly porcupion

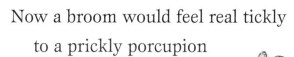

And it would seem quite scratchy
on the batchy of a lion.

What on EARTH are you talking about?
Just tell me what you do with a broom.

What does your mother do with a broom?

Hmm. That's what I thought.

What can you do
What can you do
What can you do

with a bed?

Paint it **red**!

Paint it **red**, yellow, **blue**

And paint the covers too!

Paint **purple**, orange, **brown** on it

And then jump up and down on it!

Oh, no! No! NO!

What are beds for really?

That's right!   Good night . . . sleep tight!